P9-DKF-244

Chukfi Rabbit's Big, Bad Bellyache

A Trickster Tale

told by GREG RODGERS

illustrated by
LESLIE STALL WIDENER

PAWNEE
PUBLIC
LIBRARY

Note to the Reader

You're about to learn some new names for some old familiar animals. The people who told this story a long time ago were Choctaw and so they used the Choctaw words for Rabbit, Fox, Bear, Turtle, Beaver and Possum, like this: Chukfi, Chula, Nita, Luksi, Kinta and Shukata. But they were people just like you and me and so sometimes they used the Choctaw word and sometimes they used the English name and sometimes they used them both together, just like I'm going to do in *Chukfi Rabbit's Big Bad Bellyache*. Maybe by the time you're finished with this story, you'll know the new names too.

DOWN HERE IN CHOCTAW COUNTRY most folks'll tell you that Chukfi Rabbit is lay-zeeee. And then they'll say, "And watch your food when Chukfi Rabbit is around. Blink once and it'll all be gone."

Like that one time, long ago…

Ms. Shukata Possum needed a new house. Several of her friends agreed on an everybody-work-together day to build her one. All except Chukfi Rabbit, that is.

"Chukfi? Would you like to help build me a house?" asked Ms. Possum. "Chula Fox, Nita Bear, Luksi Turtle, and Kinta Beaver will all be there."

"Oh, I'm just so sorry," said Chukfi Rabbit, "I'm much, much too busy on that day."

"But I didn't even say which day."

"Oh, which day?" asked Chukfi.

"Tomorrow."

"Yep, yep. Much, much too busy tomorrow. So sorry."

"Oh, that's too bad," said Ms. Shukata. "I'm making dinner with fresh homemade butter for everyone who helps."

"Oh, wait," said Chukfi, "I just remembered—it's the next day that I'm too busy. Tomorrow I can most certainly be there."

Well, that's just how Chukfi Rabbit is.

Early the next morning, everyone showed up at Ms. Possum's place. She had made cornbread biscuits, grape dumplings, *tanchi labona*, which is a Choctaw kind of corn stew, and—best of all—lots and lots of homemade butter. It was creamy and delicious and hard to make, a real treat. But all that food would have to wait for dinner, after the work was done.

When the working started, Kinta did the saw-saw-sawing. Chula did the dig-dig-digging for the corner posts. Ms. Shukata did the sweep-sweep-sweeping while Nita Bear and Luksi Turtle did the ham-ham-hammering. Since they didn't really have hammers back in those days, Luksi kindly agreed to be the hammer. And Rabbit? Well, as usual, Chukfi had disappeared.

Chula Fox called out, "Chukfi, where are you?"

From behind a pile of rocks, Rabbit answered, "Over here."

"Why aren't you working?" asked Chula.

"I'm sick," said Chukfi. "I have a fever. But I think it will pass soon enough, and then I'll be ready to work."

But this wasn't true at all. Rabbit wasn't sick, he was just hiding.

When no one was watching, Chukfi snuck down to the coldwater spring where the food was kept and took the tub of homemade butter. He carried it back to his hiding spot, behind the rocks.

Chukfi could hear the saw-saw-sawing
and the ham-ham-hammering. He heard Ms. Possum's
sweep-sweep-sweeping and Chula Fox's dig-dig-digging.

"This working and building could take all day," he said
to himself.

Chukfi took the lid off the tub of butter. It was full. He didn't
want to wait for supper. He wanted to taste it right now. So he
licked the top of the thick, creamy spread.

Once again, Chula called out, "Is your fever gone yet?"

Rabbit ran his tongue along his buttery lips. "Just starting," he
said. This was sort of the truth. Not about his fever, but he had *just
started* eating the butter. **Mm Mmmm!** It was *sooo* good! *Just
one more taste*, he told himself, *they'll never even notice.*

Then another, and another. He slid his paw deep into the
butter and ate whole pawfuls at a time.

After a while, Chula Fox called out again. "How about now? Has your fever run its course?"

Chukfi looked at the tub of butter. "About halfway," he answered.

The sun moved across the sky overhead. By the middle of the afternoon, Rabbit had still not started working.

"How's your fever now?" hollered Chula.

"Almost gone," said Chukfi.

Yep, that's right, the tub was nearly empty.

He scraped the last bit of butter from the bowl and slipped it into his mouth. He lay back against the rocks, his belly full.

When he could move again, he snuck down to the spring and returned the empty tub.

As the sun started down for
the end of the day, Rabbit appeared
from behind the rocks.

"Okay," he said, "I'm ready to work."

But it was too late. Ms. Shukata Possum's
new house was finished.

"Oh, I'm so sad," said Chukfi. "I missed all the work."

"That's okay," said Ms. Shukata, "at least
you're feeling better.
Now let's eat!"

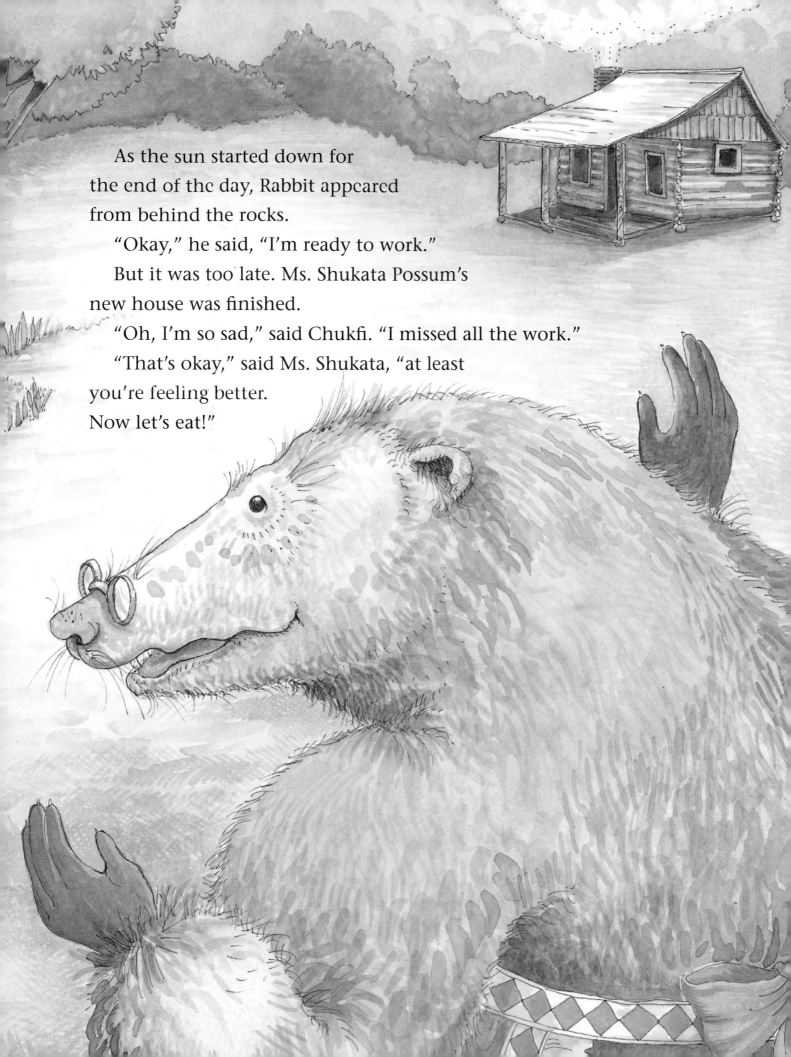

Ms. Possum spread out the food. When she opened the lid to the big tub of butter, she gasped.

"Someone ate it all!" she said, showing everyone the empty tub.

"It wasn't me," said Chukfi, "I was sick all day."

They all nodded. "That's true," said Nita Bear. "But who?"

"It could have been any of you," said Chula Fox. "All of us went down to the water to get a drink. Any one of you could have eaten the butter."

"Not me," said Nita Bear, Luksi Turtle, and Kinta Beaver at the same time.

"Well," said Ms. Shukata. "Let's just eat all this other food and I'll make some more butter another time."

And they did, eat that is. They munch-munch-munched the cornbread biscuits. They slurp-slurp-slurped the *tanchi labona*. And then they smack-smack-smacked on the grape dumplings.

Chukfi didn't want the others to know that he was already full. So even though his belly was great-big stuffed, he ate everything Ms. Shukata gave him.

PAWNEE
PUBLIC
LIBRARY

After the meal, they all lay down for a nap. While the others slept, Chukfi saw a little bit of butter still on the fur of his paw. He rubbed it gently on Nita Bear's big nose.

Then he licked his paws clean and lay down too.

When the others woke, Chukfi said, "Why don't we check everybody's nose? Whoever ate the butter might still have some left there."

One by one, Chula Fox examined their noses.

"Kinta, your nose is clean. Luksi, yours is kind of dirty, though certainly not buttery. But Nita Bear, your nose looks awful shiny—and greasy."

Nita licked her nose. "It does taste like butter, but I didn't eat it."

Poor Nita, nobody believed her. And they were mad. They pointed their fingers, paws, and claws at her. "You ate the butter," they shouted.

Chukfi had such a hard time not laughing. To him, this was *soooo* funny.

Then his tell-tale belly began to shake and tremble.

His tummy rumbled and before he could even get his paw up to cover his mouth, which is, of course, always good manners, he let out a great, big…**BRRRUUUUHPPP!**

"Oh," he said quickly, "excuse me."

But it was too late. The others had already smelled Chukfi's big, bad butter breath.

"It was you!" they all shouted. "Not Nita. *You* ate all the butter."

"Let's get him," growled Nita Bear.

Chukfi tried to hop away. But his belly was too full. He was too heavy. He tripped over his own floppy feet and rolled down the hill—all the way to the river. **SPLASH!**

But because butter is lighter than water, Chukfi floated downstream and away from the others.

Chukfi escaped, this time. And maybe, just maybe, he learned a lesson. Then again, probably not. But for the next four weeks, Chukfi Rabbit did have one really, really, big, bad bellyache.

So it was, that on this particular everybody-work-together day, nobody but Chukfi Rabbit got any butter— well, maybe Nita Bear if you count that one little lick on her nose.

But Ms. Shukata did get a nice, new house. And everybody did feel real happy about that, as helping others is **always** more joyful than even the best butter ever.

Note to Storytellers and Readers

"YOU DON'T FIND THE STORIES, the stories find you!" That's what I have always been told. And I believe it.

A few years back, I was doing some research at the Oklahoma History Center, scrolling through pages and pages of microfilmed transcriptions of old Choctaw interviews in the Oral History Archives. Though I came to the Center with specific goals—mostly looking for ancestral family names and places—I found myself stopping at random interviews and just reading. Many of them were so fascinating. I couldn't help but spend the next several hours imagining the written voices of the Choctaw past.

Then the story of Chukfi Rabbit found me!—an old story, probably transcribed in the late 1930s, hidden away for decades, calling out to be re-introduced into the living world of Choctaw literature. Through all our joys and sorrows, these stories manage to find their way back—to lift our spirits, reinforce our values, and remind us who we are as a people.

The Choctaw language links our past with our present lives and displays a distinct Choctaw worldview. Nearly two hundred years ago our language, with the help of missionaries, became a written language. Newspapers and books appeared with articles in both Choctaw and English, a practice that continues still.

Today an estimated 8,000 Choctaws speak our language fluently. Though we are a scattered people, living across the continent and the world, most of the Choctaw speakers live in Oklahoma and Mississippi, our original homeland. Both the Mississippi Band of Choctaw Indians and the Choctaw Nation of Oklahoma—two distinct governments—are determined to keep the language alive. Instruction is offered from K-12, at universities, community centers, and online. It is further promoted through immersion programs, bilingual publications, language fairs, and in the home.

Choctaw speech and its soothing rhythms reach deeply into our hearts and are a source of warm comfort to Choctaw ears—even the long, floppy ears of Chukfi Rabbit.

—Greg Rodgers

FOR MY GRANDMOTHERS, Addey Mae and Pauline, who always made time for a story. A special thank you to Tim Tingle and Ian Thompson for all their encouragement and shared knowledge! *—Greg Rodgers*

FOR MY HUSBAND, Terry. *—Leslie Widener*

Visit us at www.cincopuntos.com or call 1-915-838-1625.

Book and cover design by Vicki Trego Hill of El Paso, Texas. Printed in the U.S.A. by Versa Press.

Chukfi Rabbit's Big, Bad Bellyache: A Trickster Tale. Copyright © 2014 by Greg Rodgers. Illustrations copyright © 2014 by Leslie Stall Widener. All rights reserved. No part of this book may be used or reproduced in any manner whatsoever without written permission except in case of brief quotations for reviews. For information, write Cinco Puntos Press, 701 Texas Ave., El Paso, TX 79901 or call at (915) 838-1625. Printed in the U.S. FIRST EDITION 10 9 8 7 6 5 4 3 2 1 Library of Congress Cataloging-in-Publication Data. Rodgers, Greg. Chukfi Rabbit's big, bad bellyache : a trickster tale / told by Greg Rodgers ; illustrated by Leslie Stall Widener. — First edition.   pages cm Summary: Bear, Turtle, Fox, and Beaver agree to build Ms. Possum a new house, but Chukfi Rabbit says he is too busy to help until he hears there will be a Chocktaw feast afterwards and helps himself to a treat while the work is being done.   ISBN 978-1-935955-26-9 (hardback) — ISBN 978-1-935955-27-6 (paper). E-book ISBN 978-1-935955-60-3 1. Choctaw Indians—Folklore. 2. Rabbit (Legendary character)—Legends. I. Widener, Leslie Stall, illustrator. II. Title.   E99.C8R64 2013   398.20897'387—dc23   2013010568